**Read On**

Who Likes Pancakes?

Wes Magee

For Keira, Cameron, Guy and Zac

Copyright © QED Publishing 2005

First published in the UK in 2005 by
QED Publishing
A Quarto Group company
226 City Road
London EC1V 2TT
www.qed-publishing.co.uk

A Catalogue record for this book is available from the British Library.

ISBN 1 84538 171 8

Written by Wes Magee
Designed by Zeta Jones
Editor Hannah Ray
Illustrated by Anna Wilman

Series Consultant Anne Faundez
Publisher Steve Evans
Creative Director Louise Morley
Editorial Manager Jean Coppendale

Printed and bound in China

Who Likes Pancakes?

Wes Magee

QED Publishing

Who Likes Pancakes?

Who likes Pancakes?
Who likes Beans?
Who likes Pizza?
Who likes Greens?
Who likes Apples?
Who likes Cheese?
Who likes Pudding?
Who likes Peas?
Who likes Ice-cream
for their tea?

Mum,
　　and
　　　Dad,
　　　　and
　　　　　Gran,
　　　　　　and
　　　　　　　Me!

4

Pink Peaches

Pink peaches,

purple plums,

peaches, plums and pears.

Roll them,

roll them,

one by one

down

your

Grandad's

stairs.

HEY!

5

Here Come the Creatures

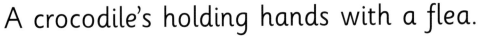

Here come the creatures.
One,
  Two,
    Three.
A crocodile's holding hands with a flea.
A tiger's arm-in-arm with a rat,
and a terrapin's toddling on with a bat.
An elephant's side-by-side with a wren,
and a warthog's waddling along with a hen.
Here come the creatures.
Eight,
  Nine,
    Ten.

6

Mad March Hare

He runs so fast
   with ears a-flopping.
    There he goes,
      and he's not stopping!

Can You ...?

Can you creep like a tortoise?
Can you zoom like a bee?
Can you swing like an ape
   in a jungle tree?

Can you hop like a rabbit?
Can you jump like a flea?
Can you swim like a shark
   in the deep blue sea?

The Best Band

"Join our band,
join our band.
We're the best band
in the land."

The trumpets toot,
and the flutes all hoot!
The cowbells clang,
and the drums all bang!
The cymbals crash,
and the blocks all bash!
The chime bars ring
and we all sing ...

"Join our band,
join our band.
We're the best band
in the land."

8

A Card for my Dad

This is the card I've made for my Dad.
  It's sticky with glue, but it's not too bad.

I've cut out a ship and stuck it in,
  and I've drawn a shark with a great big fin.

I've written as neatly as I can,
  "With love to my Dad. The world's best man!"

This is the card I'll give to my Dad.
  It's sticky with glue, but it's not too bad.

My Book of Animals

"Let's sit here and take a look
at all the animals in my book."

"See this brown bear. Bet he can growl.
And there's a tiger on the prowl."

"I like these lions in the sun,
and, hey, striped zebras on the run."

"Count the elephants. One. Two. Three.
Ha! Silly monkeys up a tree!"

"There's a camel, and there's a snake,
and here's a hippo in the lake."

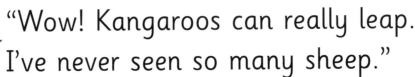

"Wow! Kangaroos can really leap.
I've never seen so many sheep."

"It's great to sit and take a look
10   at all the animals in my book."

The Rabbits' Race

Racing round the garden
Bun and Bobtail go.
Racing round the garden,
huff and puff and blow.

Racing round the garden
Bun and Bobtail run.
Racing round the garden,
in the summer sun.

But ... **who** came first?

Who won?

Drink a Glass of Lemonade

Drink a glass of lemonade.
    Gurgle,
    gurgle,
    glug.

Second glass of lemonade.
    Gurgle,
    gurgle,
    glug.

Third glass of lemonade.
Now you'd better stop.
One more glass of lemonade
    and
    you'll
    go

POP!

Six Doughnuts

Six doughnuts
in a paper bag.
Shake them round and round.

No doughnuts
in a paper bag.
They're all on the ground.

Pick them up ...

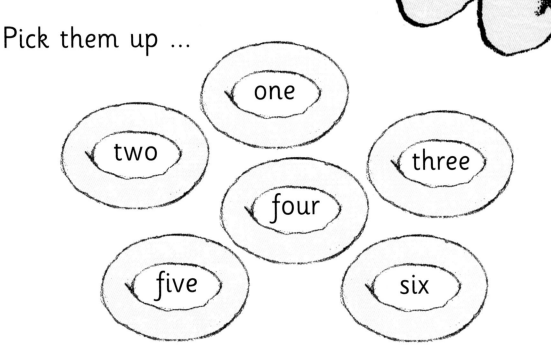

I Know a Secret Garden

I know a secret garden
  where whispering breezes blow,
    where golden fish swim in the pond
    and moonbeam flowers grow.

I know a secret garden
  where blue birds shine and glow,
where silver plums hang in the trees
and sometimes there is snow.

I know a secret garden
  where peacocks come and go,
    where chocolate cats snooze in the sun
    and singing streamlets flow.

The Waterfall

Over rugged rocks the

w
a
t
e
r
f
a
l
l

tumbles
and rumbles.

In winter
it gasps and groans
and grumbles.

But in summer
it's quiet.
It just whispers and mumbles.

In Bed with my Cuddly Creatures

Who's tucked-up
   with me in bed?
Peter Panda
   and Foxy Fred,

Ally-Gator,
   Floppy Frog,
   Tiger Tom
      and Desmond Dog,

Silly Snake
   and One-Eared Ted,
   all tucked-up
      with me in bed.

Above our Town

Above the houses
of our town
the sad-faced Moon
is gazing down.

Above the rooftops
stars so bright
are twinkling, twinkling
in the night.

The Sweeper in the Snowy Street

Snow fell silently in the night
  and now the street is frosty white.

I watch a man with snowy feet
  go slowly sweeping down the street.

His heavy boots have ice-capped toes.
  An icicle hangs from his nose.

With snow-topped hat he seems so old,
  this lonely figure in the cold.

Along the street I watch him go,
  a snowman sweeping in the snow.

18

Sam's Staying with Me

Sam is one of my friends.
Today he's feeling sad.
His mum has gone to hospital,
and Sam has got no dad.

My mum's invited Sam
to stay here in our house.
He looks upset and tearful,
and he's quiet as a mouse.

We've had fried egg and chips,
and now we'll watch TV.
While his mum's in hospital,
Sam's staying with me.

What do you think?

Read the poem 'Who Likes Pancakes?' What is your favourite food?

Look at 'Here Come the Creatures'. Which is the biggest creature? Which is the smallest creature?

Can you remember which instrument in 'The Best Band' went 'toot'?

How many doughnuts ended up on the ground? Can you count them?

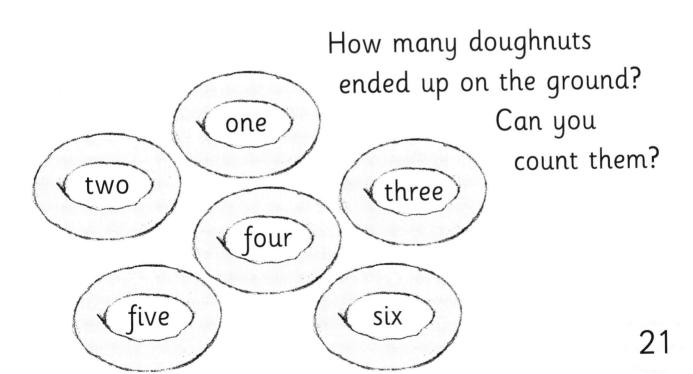

one

two

three

four

five

six

What would you like to find
in a secret garden?

How many cuddly
creatures can
you remember?

Why was Sam sad?

Was a snowman really sweeping the street? What do you think?

23

Parents' and teachers' notes

- Together, memorize, and then recite, the poem 'Who Likes Pancakes?' (page 4).
- Read 'Pink Peaches' (page 5) aloud and encourage your child to clap along with the rhythm. End the poem by shouting 'Hey!' together, with your hands raised in the air.
- Read 'Here Come the Creatures' (page 6). Can your child identify each of the creatures in the illustration?
- Read the poem 'Can You …?' (page 7). Encourage your child to act out (or mime) each line e.g. creeping like a tortoise, jumping like a flea, etc.
- Using real (or homemade) percussion instruments, add sound effects to 'The Best Band' (page 8). Try reading the poem aloud, with your child adding a percussion noise at the end of each line, and perhaps a cacophony of instrumental noise to finish!
- Together, read 'The Rabbits' Race' (page 11). Encourage your child to talk about other pets. What do different pets eat? What sounds do they make? Where do they sleep?
- Read 'Six Doughnuts' (page 13). Ask your child to act it out as you read. Can he or she look surprised when the bag rips? Can he or she mime picking the doughnuts up again and placing them in an imaginary bag?
- Read 'I Know a Secret Garden' (page 14). Ask your child to imagine that he or she knows a secret garden, and to describe it.
- After you have read 'Above our Town' (page 17), allow your child to paint a picture of the night sky. Using white paint on black sugar paper, he or she can paint a moon (with a face) and add stars, planets and even a spaceship!
- Read 'The Sweeper in the Snowy Street' (page 18) and talk with your child about making a snowman. He or she can then draw a picture of the snowman, complete with hat, carrot nose, coal eyes and a scarf.
- Talk about the poem 'Sam's Staying with Me' (page 19). Why is Sam sad? How would your child cheer up Sam if Sam was staying in your home?